W9-AVJ-802

THE DARK KNIGHT RISES™

HarperFestival is an imprint of
HarperCollins Publishers.

HARP5006
Printed in the United States of America. No part of this book
may be used or reproduced in any manner whatsoever without
written permission except in the case of brief quotations
embodied in critical articles and reviews. For information address
HarperCollins Children's Books, a division of HarperCollins
Publishers, 10 East 53rd Street, New York, NY 10022.
www.harpercollinschildrens.com

Library of Congress catalog card number: 2011945730
ISBN 978-0-06-213221-5

Book design by John Sazaklis

12 13 14 15 16 CWM 10 9 8 7 6 5 4 3 2 1
❖
First Edition

THE DARK KNIGHT RISES™

BATMAN
VERSUS
CATWOMAN

ADAPTED BY **LUCY ROSEN**

ILLUSTRATED BY **ANDY SMITH**

DIGITAL COLORS BY **JEREMY ROBERTS**

INSPIRED BY THE FILM **THE DARK KNIGHT RISES**
SCREENPLAY BY **JONATHAN NOLAN** AND **CHRISTOPHER NOLAN**
STORY BY **CHRISTOPHER NOLAN** AND **DAVID S. GOYER**
BATMAN CREATED BY **BOB KANE**

HARPER FESTIVAL

An Imprint of HarperCollinsPublishers

Wayne Manor glowed against Gotham City's dark sky. Bruce Wayne's famous mansion was buzzing with the sounds of a party. Between bites of fancy food, the city's richest citizens talked about Gotham's latest trouble.

"Have you heard about the cat burglar?" said one guest. "This robber has been stealing om every wealthy person in town! I hope your house is secure, Bruce."

Bruce smiled slightly. "I'm not too worried about that," he said, helping himself to a snack.

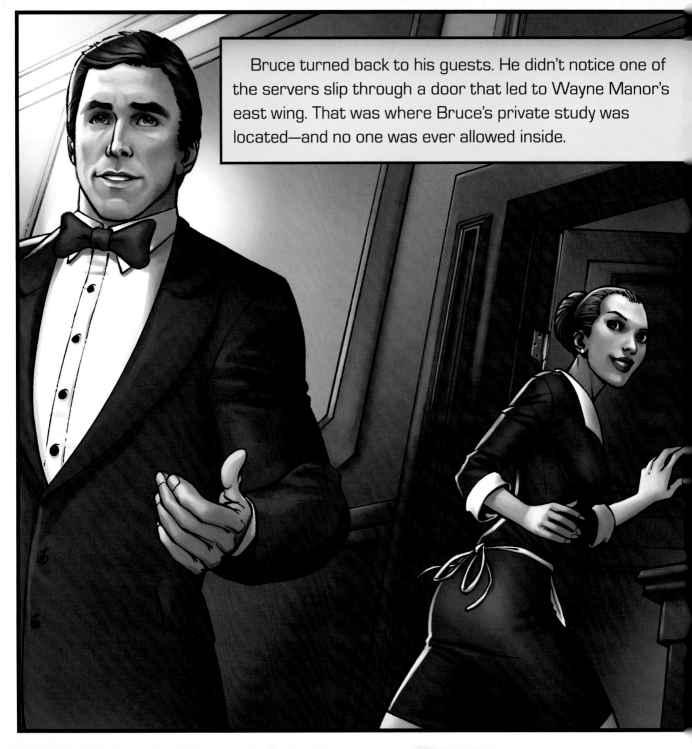

Bruce turned back to his guests. He didn't notice one of the servers slip through a door that led to Wayne Manor's east wing. That was where Bruce's private study was located—and no one was ever allowed inside.

The woman glided into the study, hardly making a sound. In no time, she had found Bruce's hidden safe and opened it expertly with her tool kit.

"What a beauty," the burglar gasped as she removed what was inside: a delicate pearl necklace that once belonged to Bruce's mother, Martha. "You're coming with me," she said, pocketing the priceless belonging.

"Not so fast," a voice boomed in the doorway. It was Bruce!
A silent alarm had told him that someone was breaking in.

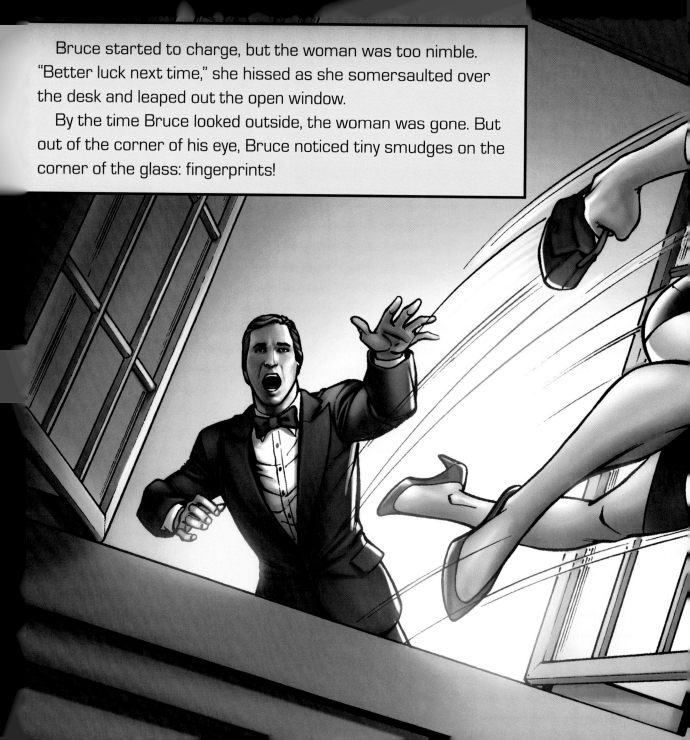

Bruce started to charge, but the woman was too nimble. "Better luck next time," she hissed as she somersaulted over the desk and leaped out the open window.

By the time Bruce looked outside, the woman was gone. But out of the corner of his eye, Bruce noticed tiny smudges on the corner of the glass: fingerprints!

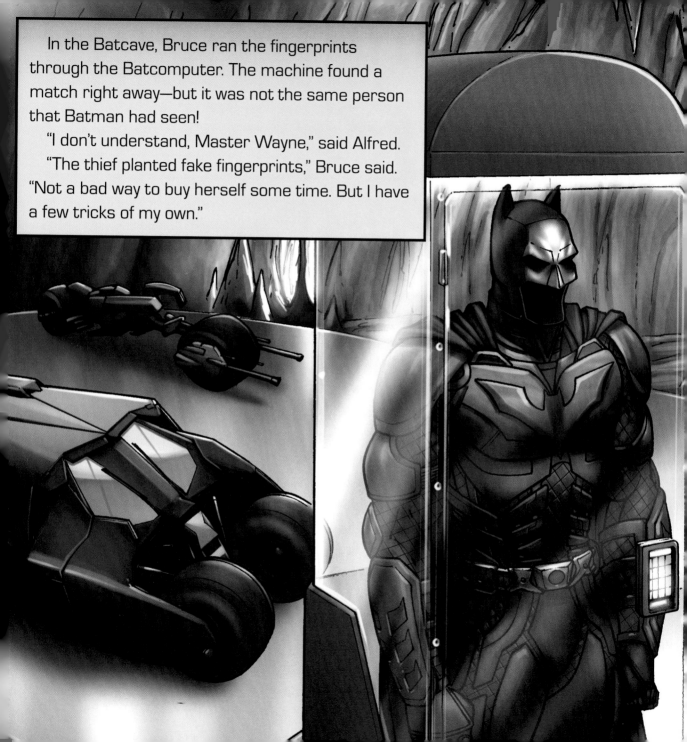

In the Batcave, Bruce ran the fingerprints through the Batcomputer. The machine found a match right away—but it was not the same person that Batman had seen!

"I don't understand, Master Wayne," said Alfred.

"The thief planted fake fingerprints," Bruce said. "Not a bad way to buy herself some time. But I have a few tricks of my own."

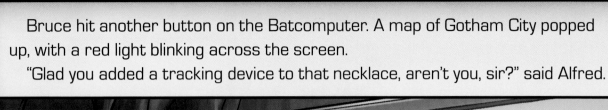

Bruce hit another button on the Batcomputer. A map of Gotham City popped up, with a red light blinking across the screen.

"Glad you added a tracking device to that necklace, aren't you, sir?" said Alfred.

KYLE, SELINA

The Gotham Times

CAT BURGLAR STRIKES AGAIN

PRICELESS JEWELS STOLEN!

The necklace was in the hands of a woman named Selina Kyle—a wanted jewel thief and the burglar who was robbing Gotham City's rich. Bruce found article after article about Selina's many crimes.

"Looks like I've got cat trouble," Bruce told Alfred.

The next night, Bruce tracked the signal to the Gotham City museum.

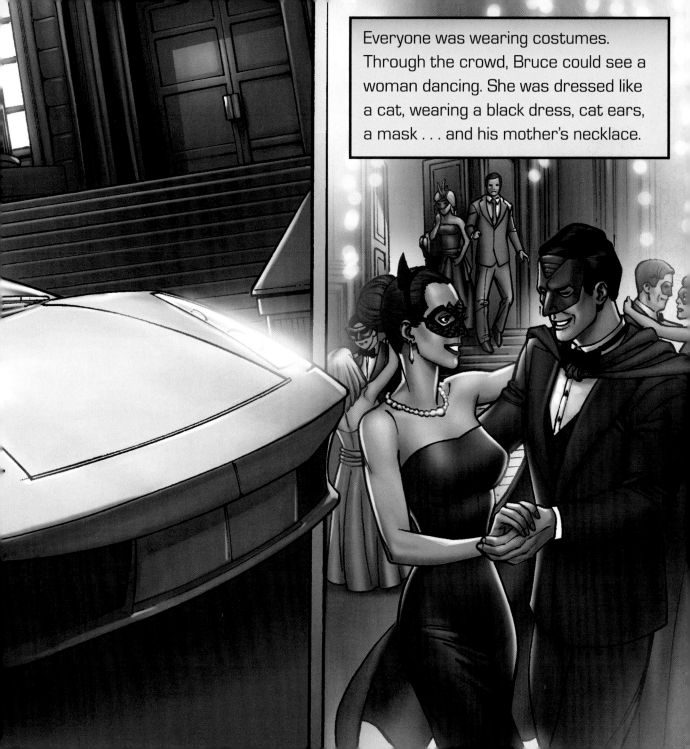

Everyone was wearing costumes. Through the crowd, Bruce could see a woman dancing. She was dressed like a cat, wearing a black dress, cat ears, a mask . . . and his mother's necklace.

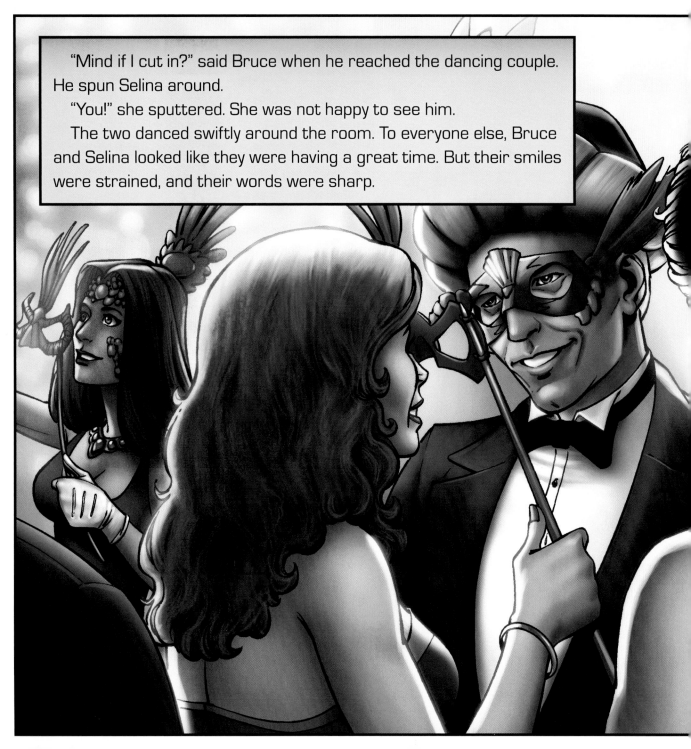

"Mind if I cut in?" said Bruce when he reached the dancing couple. He spun Selina around.

"You!" she sputtered. She was not happy to see him.

The two danced swiftly around the room. To everyone else, Bruce and Selina looked like they were having a great time. But their smiles were strained, and their words were sharp.

"What's the matter?" Bruce asked Selina, gliding her across the dance floor. "Cat got your tongue?" "No," Selina snapped. "Cat's got your necklace."

"Not for long," said Bruce. He pushed one arm away, forcing Selina to spin around. Before she could regain her balance, Bruce dipped her— and quickly unhooked the necklace.

Back on her feet, Selina shoved Bruce out of her way. She dashed out of the ballroom before he could catch her.

"She won't get away that easily," Bruce thought, running after her. "I'll chase her down in my car." As he ran down the museum steps, Bruce fumbled with his pockets. Where were his car keys?

The roar of an engine got Bruce's attention. Selina Kyle waved out of the window of a sleek silver sports car— *Bruce's* silver sports car.

"Like I said," she called, "better luck next time!"

Bruce vowed that the next time Catwoman crossed his path, Batman would be ready.